GOSCINNY AND UDERZO

PRESENT
An Asterix Adventure

ASTERIX
IN
BELGIUM

Written by RENÉ GOSCINNY *and Illustrated by* ALBERT UDERZO

Translated by Anthea Bell *and* Derek Hockridge

with apologies to:
George Gordon, Lord Byron,
Mr Wm. Shakespeare, Mr John Milton
and Pieter Breughel the Elder

Asterix titles available now

© 1979 GOSCINNY/UDERZO
Revised edition and English translation © 2004 Hachette Livre
Original title: *Astérix chez les Belges*

Exclusive licensee: Orion Publishing Group
Translators: Anthea Bell and Derek Hockridge
Typography: Bryony Newhouse

This revised edition first published in 2004 by Orion Books Ltd,
Orion House, 5 Upper Saint Martin's Lane, London WC2H 9EA
An Hachette UK company

5 7 9 10 8 6 4

Printed in China

www.asterix.com
www.orionbooks.co.uk

A CIP record for this book is available from the British Library

ISBN 978-0-7528-6649-9 (cased)
ISBN 978-0-7528-6650-5 (paperback)

The Orion Publishing Group's policy is to use papers that are natural, renewable and recyclable products
and made from wood grown in sustainable forests. The logging and manufacturing processes are
expected to conform to the environmental regulations of the country of origin.

BELGICA

GAULISH VILLAGE

COMPENDIUM

LAUDANUM

AQUARIUM

TOTORUM

ARMORICA

LUTETIA

SPQR

GAUL
(ROMAN CONQUEST)
50 BC

CELTICA

AQUITANIA

PROVINCIA

THE YEAR IS 50 BC. GAUL IS ENTIRELY OCCUPIED BY THE
ROMANS. WELL, NOT ENTIRELY ... ONE SMALL VILLAGE OF
INDOMITABLE GAULS STILL HOLDS OUT AGAINST THE INVADERS.
AND LIFE IS NOT EASY FOR THE ROMAN LEGIONARIES WHO
GARRISON THE FORTIFIED CAMPS OF TOTORUM, AQUARIUM,
LAUDANUM AND COMPENDIUM ...

ASTERIX, THE HERO OF THESE ADVENTURES. A SHREWD, CUNNING LITTLE WARRIOR, ALL PERILOUS MISSIONS ARE IMMEDIATELY ENTRUSTED TO HIM. ASTERIX GETS HIS SUPERHUMAN STRENGTH FROM THE MAGIC POTION BREWED BY THE DRUID GETAFIX . . .

OBELIX, ASTERIX'S INSEPARABLE FRIEND. A MENHIR DELIVERY MAN BY TRADE, ADDICTED TO WILD BOAR. OBELIX IS ALWAYS READY TO DROP EVERYTHING AND GO OFF ON A NEW ADVENTURE WITH ASTERIX – SO LONG AS THERE'S WILD BOAR TO EAT, AND PLENTY OF FIGHTING. HIS CONSTANT COMPANION IS DOGMATIX, THE ONLY KNOWN CANINE ECOLOGIST, WHO HOWLS WITH DESPAIR WHEN A TREE IS CUT DOWN.

GETAFIX, THE VENERABLE VILLAGE DRUID, GATHERS MISTLETOE AND BREWS MAGIC POTIONS. HIS SPECIALITY IS THE POTION WHICH GIVES THE DRINKER SUPERHUMAN STRENGTH. BUT GETAFIX ALSO HAS OTHER RECIPES UP HIS SLEEVE . . .

CACOFONIX, THE BARD. OPINION IS DIVIDED AS TO HIS MUSICAL GIFTS. CACOFONIX THINKS HE'S A GENIUS. EVERY-ONE ELSE THINKS HE'S UNSPEAKABLE. BUT SO LONG AS HE DOESN'T SPEAK, LET ALONE SING, EVERYBODY LIKES HIM . . .

FINALLY, VITALSTATISTIX, THE CHIEF OF THE TRIBE. MAJESTIC, BRAVE AND HOT-TEMPERED, THE OLD WARRIOR IS RESPECTED BY HIS MEN AND FEARED BY HIS ENEMIES. VITALSTATISTIX HIMSELF HAS ONLY ONE FEAR, HE IS AFRAID THE SKY MAY FALL ON HIS HEAD TOMORROW. BUT AS HE ALWAYS SAYS, TOMORROW NEVER COMES.

5

A REST CURE?

THEY'RE SENDING ROMANS HERE FOR A REST CURE?

AND THE LEGIONARY TOLD US THAT AFTER THE BELGIANS, EVEN OBELIX THUMPING HIM WAS LOVELY.

AND THEY KEEP TELLING FUNNY STORIES ABOUT BELGIANS. THERE WAS ONE ABOUT KNOCKING NAILS INTO WALLS WITH THEIR HANDS, THE WAY I ALWAYS DO!

THERE'S NO NEED TO GET UPSET; I THINK IT'S RATHER PLEASING TO KNOW THE ROMANS COME HERE FOR A REST CURE.

RATHER PLEASING?

IF THIS SORT OF THING GOES ON, WE'LL HAVE EVERYONE COMING TO THE ARMORICAN COAST FOR THEIR HOLIDAYS TO ENJOY THE BRACING AIR, THE COUNTRYSIDE, THE FOOD...

WE'RE TURNING INTO A HOLIDAY CAMP FOR ROMANS, AND HE THINKS IT'S RATHER PLEASING! MAKES YOU WONDER IF IT WAS WORTH FIGHTING THE BATTLE OF GERGOVIA AT ALL!

DON'T GET SO UPSET, PIGGYWIGGY. IT WAS ONLY A COMMON LEGIONARY'S OPINION. JULIUS CAESAR VALUES YOU AT YOUR TRUE WORTH.

THE FACT IS...

THE FACT IS WHAT?

JULIUS CAESAR SAID THE BELGIANS WERE THE BRAVEST OF ALL THE GAULISH PEOPLES.

OH, SO THAT'S WHAT CAESAR SAID, IS IT? RIGHT, YOU KNOW WHAT I THINK OF CAESAR?

PIGGYWIGGY, IF YOU WANT TO BE COARSE, GO AND BE COARSE ELSEWHERE!

YOU BET I WILL! I'M CALLING A VILLAGE COUNCIL MEETING STRAIGHT AWAY!

I'VE SUMMONED YOU BECAUSE I'M FED TO THE TEETH WITH HEARING ABOUT THESE BELGIANS CAESAR THINKS ARE SO BRAVE...

OH, I THOUGHT YOU'D SUMMONED US TO FEED US TO THE TEETH WITH WILD BOAR...

LOOK, WE'RE ONLY JUST STARTING THIS STORY. IT'S MUCH TOO SOON FOR THE BANQUET, AND ANYWAY, THE BARD IS STILL WITH US.

SHUT UP, YOU TWO CLOWNS! I SUGGEST WE GO AND SEE THESE BELGIANS AND FIND OUT WHAT'S SO SPECIAL ABOUT THEM!

BONK!

AND THEN WE'LL SHOW THEM WE'RE THE BRAVEST. AND CAESAR, TOO! WHAT DO YOU THINK OF THAT?

NOT A LOT.

6A

IF THE BELGIANS ARE BRAVE, GOOD FOR THEM AND TOO BAD FOR CAESAR. WE'D DO BETTER TO MIND OUR OWN BUSINESS!

GETAFIX IS RIGHT! ARTISTIC VALUES MATTER MORE THAN BRUTE FORCE. I MEAN, LOOK AT ME...

MY WIFE DOESN'T LIKE ME TO GO AWAY ON MY OWN... SHE HAS SUCH A JEALOUS NATURE!

PERSONALLY, I AGREE WITH THE DRUID.

RIGHT, SO THAT'S THE END OF THE STORY, AND WE CAN TIE UP THE BARD AND BRING ON THE BOAR!

WELL, IF THAT'S HOW YOU FEEL, I'M OFF TO SEE THE BELGIANS ON MY OWN!

I'LL SHOW EVERYONE THAT THE BRAVEST OF ALL THE GAULISH PEOPLES IS ME!

I THINK YOU AND OBELIX HAD BETTER GO WITH HIM, OR THIS STORY MAY COME TO A STICKY AS WELL AS A PREMATURE END.

6B

SO WHAT'S THE BIG JOKE, AND WHO ARE YOU JOKERS, ANYWAY?

I'M A VETERAN OF GERGOVIA. WE'RE FROM ARMORICA, AND...

ARMORICANS.

THOUGHT SO, FROM THEIR ARMORICANISMS.

AND YOU'RE BELGIANS?

THAT'S RIGHT. YOU'RE LIKELY TO MEET BELGIANS IN BELGIUM.

WE'RE DIVIDED INTO BELLOVACI, SUESSIONES, EBURONES, ATUATUCI, NERVII, CEUTRONES, GRUDII, LEVACI, PLEUMOXII, GELDUMNES, AND MENAPII, BUT WE'RE ALL BELGIANS.

I HEAR YOU'RE AT WAR?

AFTER WEEKS BENEATH THE CONQUEROR'S YOKE, WE DECIDED WE WEREN'T STANDING FOR IT ANY MORE!

WELL, WE'LL BE ON OUR WAY. THERE'S A ROMAN CAMP TO BE RASED TO THE GROUND BEFORE DINNER.

CAN WE COME WITH YOU?

YOU WANT TO COME AND WATCH? WHAT FOR? YOU NEED LESSONS?

LESSONS?

WE DON'T NEED ANY LESSONS FROM ANYONE!!!

ALL RIGHT, BUT YOU MUSTN'T GET IN OUR WAY. YOU AND YOUR MEN STAY AT THE BACK WHERE IT ISN'T DANGEROUS.

CRAAASH!

IT iS A TRiCK!
IT iS A TRiCK!

SLAP! SLAP! SLAP! SLAP!

I FEEL QUITE AT HOME HERE. THEIR LEGIONARIES ARE JUST LIKE OURS.

PAF!

SOON AFTERWARDS...

WELL... I THINK THAT'S OVER.

ALREADY? BUT WE'VE ONLY JUST BEGUN!

HAVE THEY GONE?

SSH! KEEP STILL.

COME ON, BOYS! I CAN'T WAIT TO SEE THE BELGIANS' FACES.

WELL, HOW DID YOU LIKE THAT, BELGIANS?

NOT BAD. QUITE AMUSING.

WHAT DO YOU MEAN, QUITE AMUSING?

WELL, COMING?

WE DON'T LIKE TO IMPOSE ON YOU...

TRUE GAULISH GALLANTRY! BUT IT'S NO TROUBLE... YOU'LL JUST GET POT LUCK. THE ROAST BOAR OF OLD BELGIUM... NONE OF YOUR FANCY LUTETIAN COOKING HERE!

RIGHT. AVE. SEE YOU SOON.

?

NOT MUCH IN THE WAY OF LANDSCAPE FEATURES HERE!

NO, THE ONLY HILLS IN OUR FLAT COUNTRYSIDE ARE CALLED OPPIDUMS.

HERE'S THE VILLAGE.

IT'S VERY LIKE OURS!

LADIES, WE HAVE VISITORS! LET'S LAY ON THE WHOLE WORKS! BURNISH UP THE BRASS! PUT ON YOUR BEST BIBS AND TUCKERS!

YES, THIS IS A REAL HOME FROM HOME, COMPLETE WITH REAL ROMANS FROM ROME!

AND THE STRANGE COMPETITION GOES ON. TRYING TO CHALK UP AS MANY VICTORIES AS POSSIBLE SO AS TO COME OUT THE WINNERS, THE GAULS AND THE BELGIANS SPREAD TERROR THROUGH THE LOCAL ROMAN FORTIFIED CAMPS.

WE JUST WANTED TO LET YOU KNOW THAT WE'RE FROM ARMORICA.

DIDN'T YOUR MOTHER EVER TEACH YOU HOW TO INTRODUCE YOURSELF POLITELY?

YOU CAN TELL CAESAR WE'RE BELGIAN.

I'M SURE HE'LL JUST LOVE THAT NEWS.

SEE THIS BOARD? WE'RE NEUTRALS, AND...

AND THE WHOLE BUNCH OF YOU ARE AS NUTTY AS THEY COME!!!

YOU'RE ARMORICANS? HOW MADLY INTERESTING!

23-A

OH, YOU'RE BELGIAN, ARE YOU? PLEASED TO MEET YOU, I'M SURE. MY REGARDS TO YOUR GOOD LADY.

AND HERS TO YOU, TOO.

I HAVEN'T THE FAINTEST IDEA WHO'S GOING TO PAY FOR YOUR SHIP! KINDLY LEAVE ME ALONE! I'VE HAD A HARD DAY'S FIGHT AS IT IS!!!

TAPTAPTAP!

WELL, WE'VE DESTROYED ALL THE CAMPS ON OUR SIDE OF THE VILLAGE, SO WE CAN GO BACK.

OH YES... I'M SURE WE'LL BE IN TIME FOR... WELL, FOR WHATEVER MEAL THEY HAVE AT THIS TIME OF DAY!

I DOUBT WHETHER THE BELGIANS HAVE DONE AS WELL AS US, BOYS! THEY'LL HAVE TO ADMIT WE'RE THE BRAVEST, EVEN WITHOUT CAESAR'S RULING!

23B

* BRASSICA OLERACEA BOTRYTIS

34

LATER...

CAESAR'S CAMP!

AVE, CAESAR! TWO MEN ARE OUTSIDE THE CAMP WITH SOMETHING BEARING A VAGUE RESEMBLANCE TO A FLAG OF TRUCE.

GO AND SEE WHAT THEY WANT. IF THEY'RE REALLY CARRYING A FLAG OF TRUCE BRING THEM TO ME.

WHAT, ME?

YES, YOU! SINCE WHEN HAS A ROMAN LEGIONARY KNOWN FEAR?

PERSONALLY, IT'LL HAVE BEEN SINCE ABOUT THREE MONTHS AGO, WHEN I ARRIVED IN BELGIUM...

...BUT I HEAR AND OBEY, O CAESAR. AVE! MORITURUS TE SALUTO, AND I WISH I COULD HAVE HAD TIME TO WRITE TO MY WIFE.

A FEW MOMENTS LATER...

HA...HALT!

PAF!

WHY DID YOU DO THAT? WE'RE CARRYING A FLAG OF TRUCE.

WELL, IT ISN'T A REAL FLAG. IT'S RIDDLED WITH HOLES.

THAT'S NO REASON TO KNOCK HIM DOWN AS IF WE WANTED TO PICK HOLES IN HIM, TOO!

PREPARATIONS FOR THE GREAT BATTLE BEGIN...

LEGATE WOLFGANGAMADEUS, ONCE BATTLE HAS BEEN JOINED YOU AND YOUR COHORTS ATTACK THE ENEMY IN THE REAR!

I HEAR AND OBEY, O CAESAR. I'LL BE OFF.

UMBELLIFERUS, I AM PUTTING YOU IN CHARGE OF MY IMPERIAL GUARD. THEY WILL TAKE PART ONLY IN THE LAST RESORT. WE SHALL OPEN FIRE WITH OUR CATAPULTS!

MAY THE GODS LOOK DOWN UPON US WITH FAVOUR!

ALEA JACTA EST!

AND AS FOR YOU, I'LL SEE YOU IN MY OFFICE AFTER THE BATTLE!

THE BELGIANS ARE GETTING READY FOR BATTLE TOO. FAST RUNNERS ARE SENT TO ROUSE THE NEIGHBOURING TRIBES...

BONANZA, DID YOU TRY THAT IDEA OF MINE ABOUT FRIED CHIPPED ROOTS?

NO, THE MENAPII INSISTED ON COOKING THE LAST MEAL BEFORE THE BATTLE. THEY WANTED A NICE WATERZOOI TO SOUP THEM UP.

WATERZOOI! WATERY STUFF FOR MEN WHO WANT CAESAR TO MEET HIS WATERLOO!

WITH JULIUS CAESAR AT THEIR HEAD, MARSHALLED IN PERFECT ORDER, THE LEGIONS, MAINTAINING STRICT MILITARY STANDARDS, MARCH OFF TO THE BATTLEFIELD.

AND POURING FORWARD WITH NOT VERY IMPETUOUS SPEED...

BY JUPITER, LEGATE WOLFGANGAMADEUS, DO YOU HAVE MUCH STOMACH FOR THIS FIGHT?

YOU BET I DO! WHAT ARE YOU BELLYACHING ABOUT?

I DON'T TRUST THESE BELGIANS, AND OUR MEN AREN'T TOO HAPPY EITHER. I'M AFRAID WE MAY BE LURED INTO A TRAP.

SO THEY'VE CHUCKED US OUT! OH, OF COURSE WE'RE ONLY FOREIGNERS, AREN'T WE? WE DON'T HAVE ANY RIGHT TO OUR BIT OF FUN! TALK ABOUT XENOPHOBIA!

DO CALM DOWN...

EVER SINCE THE START I'VE BEEN TELLING YOU THIS IS NONE OF OUR BUSINESS. SURELY YOU KNOW HOW THEY FEEL?

ALL I KNOW IS THAT I WANT TO BASH SOMEONE OVER THE HEAD! IT'S ALL VERY WELL BEING TACTFUL, BUT IF I CAN'T BASH SOMEONE OVER...

SSH!

I THINK YOU MAY BE ABLE TO LET OFF STEAM AFTER ALL; THERE ARE ROMANS COMING!

THERE, SEE THAT? YOU CAN RELY ON THE ROMANS! THE ROMANS TAKE LIFE SERIOUSLY.

LOTS OF ROMANS TOO! WE'D BETTER FINISH UP OUR MAGIC POTION.

GLUG. GLUG. GLUG.

GLUG. GLUG. GLUG.

WE'LL MEET THEM IN THAT LITTLE WOOD OVER THERE...

41

BUT YESTERDAY THE WORD OF CAESAR MIGHT HAVE STOOD AGAINST THE WORLD... HOWEVER, THAT DAY HE DID NOT OVERCOME THE NERVII, OR THE MENAPII, OR ANYBODY ELSE. CAESAR IS NO LONGER IN A POSITION TO JUDGE ANYTHING...

IN FACT, **CHAOS UMPIRE SITS**, AS THE OCCUPYING FORCES SOON REALISE:

FAREWELL, CAESAR! OUR OCCUPATION'S GONE!!!

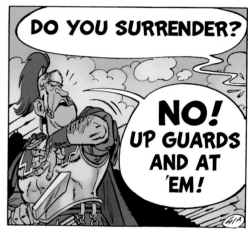

DO YOU SURRENDER?

NO! UP GUARDS AND AT 'EM!

OH NO, WE DON'T!

THESE ROMANS ARE CRAZY!

BUT UP GUARDS AND...

YOU KNOW WHAT THE GUARD WILL BE PUBLISHING TO THE WORLD ABOUT YOU?

PUBLISH AND BE DAMNED.

RIGHT. I'M BACK OFF TO ROME. I'M RELYING ON YOU TO KEEP THIS LITTLE AFFAIR AS QUIET AS POSSIBLE...

A HORSE FOR CAESAR.

AND IT IS A CASE OF **RUIN UPON RUIN, ROUT ON ROUT, CONFUSION WORSE CONFOUNDED**...

RUN FOR YOUR LIVES! RUN! RUN FOR IT!

WE'RE THE GREATEST RUN-MAKERS! WE WON THE MATCH! THEY'LL NEED MORE THAN RUNNING REPAIRS AFTER THIS!

THE WAY'S BARRED.

IF YOU INTEND TO KILL ME, BARBARIANS, I WARN YOU THAT I SHALL SELL MY DISTINGUISHED LIFE DEARLY!

NO, THAT'S NOT THE IDEA AT ALL...

IT'S ABOUT OUR COMPETITION...

YOU'VE SEEN US IN ACTION, SO NOW WILL YOU ADJUDICATE? WHO ARE THE BRAVEST?

I'VE NO IDEA WHO ARE THE BRAVEST! ALL I KNOW IS THAT YOU'RE ALL EQUALLY CRAZY!!!

AND NOW I'M GOING BACK TO ROME, AND I DON'T WANT TO BE BOTHERED ANY MORE! OFF WE GO!

? !

PFFFFF PFFFFFF

HAHAHA! HOHOHO!

COME ON BACK TO THE VILLAGE, AND WE'LL HAVE A LITTLE PARTY TO CELEBRATE!

WHAT ON EARTH IS THAT?

NO IDEA... A SOUVENIR I PICKED UP ON THE BATTLEFIELD!

LOOKS LIKE A SEASIDE SOUVENIR ... IT EVEN HAS MUSSELS STILL STICKING TO IT.

MUSSELS... THAT'S FISHY... FISH... WONDER HOW FISH WOULD GO WITH CHIPPED ROOT VEGETABLES?

AND THERE IS A SOUND OF
REVELRY BY NIGHT.

GOSCINNY & UDERZO.